Traction Man
Is Here!
MINI GREY

ALFRED A. KNOPF

New York

Traction Man is here!
(Wearing Combat Boots,
        Battle Pants, and his
                Warfare Shirt.)

Traction Man is guarding some toast.

Now who's going to help with the washing up?

He volunteers for a Special Mission.

Traction Man is diving in the foamy waters
of the Sink (wearing his Sub-Aqua Suit,
Fluorescent Flippers, and Infra-Red Mask).

He is searching for the
Lost Wreck of the Sieve.

"Well done, Scrubbing Brush! You can be my pet!"

Just ten minutes, remember...

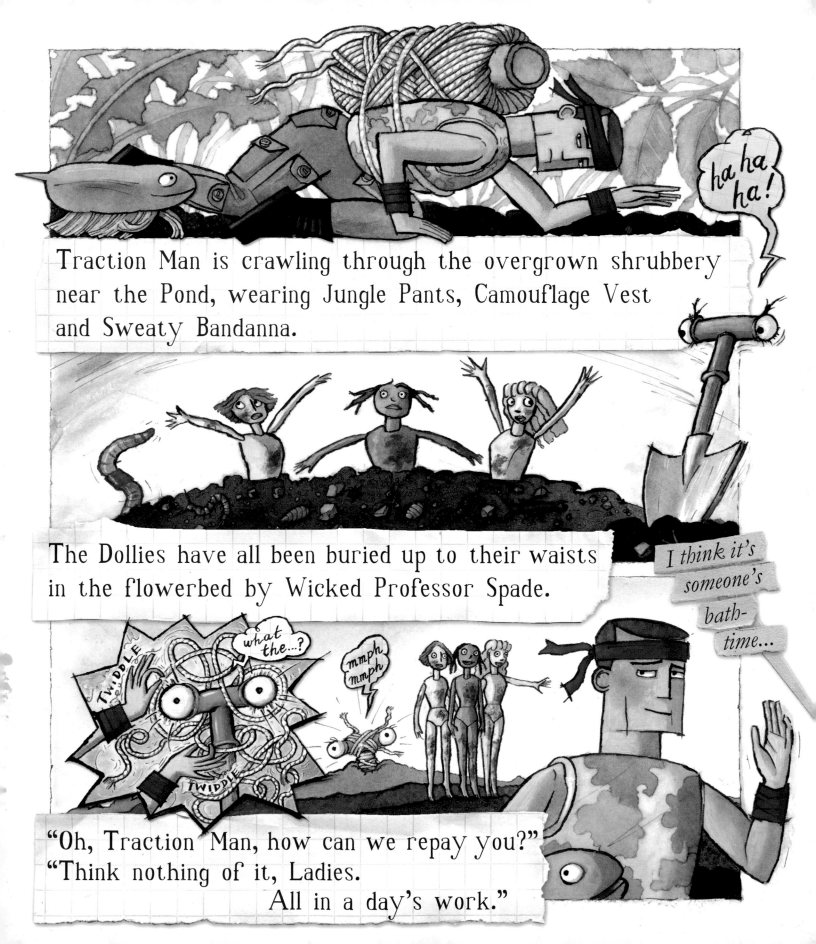

Traction Man is crawling through the overgrown shrubbery near the Pond, wearing Jungle Pants, Camouflage Vest and Sweaty Bandanna.

The Dollies have all been buried up to their waists in the flowerbed by Wicked Professor Spade.

"Oh, Traction Man, how can we repay you?"
"Think nothing of it, Ladies.
                    All in a day's work."

Traction Man and Scrubbing Brush are in the Giant InterGalactic People Mover.

They are counting Christmas trees.

They are put into suspended animation for some of the journey.

At last!
Granny's!

Oh! How lovely (grrrr).
An all-in-one knitted green romper suit
and matching bonnet!

Traction Man is sitting on the edge of the Kitchen Cliff
(wondering how long he will have to wear his all-in-one knitted
green romper suit and matching bonnet).

"Oh, **DO** be quiet, Scrubbing Brush."

My goodness! Down there!
    All those Spoons have crashed! They must be helped—
but how? The Kitchen Cliff is very high.

Traction Man and **Scrubbing Brush**
are relaxing after their latest mission,
lying comfortably on a book
in the huge blue expanse
of the Carpet.

Traction Man is wearing his
knitted Green Swimming Pants
and matching Swimming Bonnet.

They are both wearing their medals.

And they know they are ready
for **Anything.**

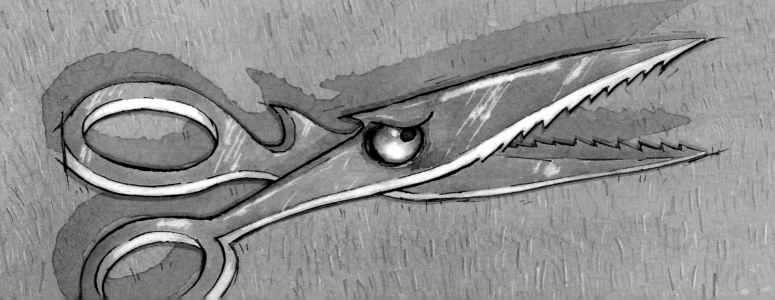

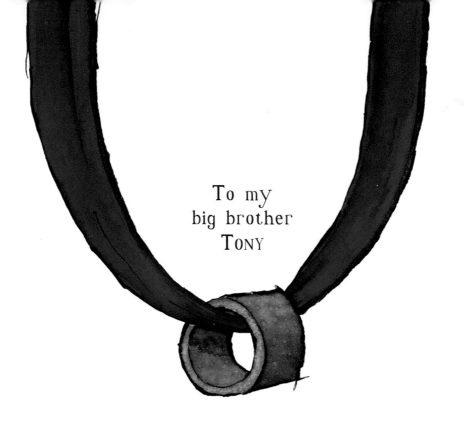

To my
big brother
TONY

THIS IS A BORZOI BOOK PUBLISHED BY ALFRED A. KNOPF

Copyright © 2005 by Mini Grey

www.randomhouse.com/kids

Library of Congress Cataloging-in-Publication Data
Grey, Mini.
Traction Man is here! / Mini Grey. — 1st American ed.
p.   cm.
SUMMARY: Traction Man, a boy's courageous action figure,
has a variety of adventures with Scrubbing Brush and
other objects in the house.
ISBN 0-375-83191-6 (trade)
ISBN 0-375-93191-0 (lib. bdg.)
[1. Action figures (Toys)—Fiction. 2. Toys—Fiction.
3. Brooms and brushes—Fiction.] I. Title.
PZ7.G873Tr 2005
[E]—dc22
2004004452

MANUFACTURED IN MALAYSIA
April 2005
10 9 8 7 6 5 4 3 2 1

E
G

Grey, Mini.

Traction Man is
here!

$17.99

DATE